How the Giraffe got his Spots

By Sandra Joanne Forder

Illustrations by Rhiannon Gower

Published by East Anglian Press

British Library Cataloguing in Publication Data.
A CIP catalogue record for this book is available from the British Library.

ISBN: 978-1-9997117-0-2

For Paul, Lauren and Haydn.

With love. xxx

Long, long ago; when the wind whispered through the Serengeti without a care in the world, there lived a giraffe.

But not the type of animal we know today.

Instead, with its head kissed by the clouds, the corn-yellow giraffe strode across the plains in search of tender treetops. He was a lonesome creature.

Being so tall meant only the birds could talk to him without trouble, but as he was so unusual to look at, they didn't bother.

The giraffe, who was called Umberto, had another problem. Unlike most animals that ate in the day and then slept all night, Umberto ate all day, and all night too.

Down in the grass two mischievous Meerkats tumbled around in the scrub. They were such a troublesome pair; they often found themselves in bother with their elders.

One night, while the world slept, the playful pair crept out of their burrow. Rolling around in the undergrowth, they were stopped by a rustling overhead. In the sky, the moon shone brightly. One Meerkat looked at the other.

'What's that noise?'

The other stood on its hind legs and scanned the savannah. Horrified, he whispered,

'Something is eating the moon!'

Savannah: This is an area of grassland and woods. They have tall grasses, and scattered trees.

Sure enough, from where the small creature sat, it did indeed look as though someone was eating the moon.

And that someone?

Umberto stooped, his dark eyes framed by glorious lashes.

Seeing the moon muncher bending towards them, the meddlesome Meerkats scrambled back into their burrow, afraid that they would be next on the menu.

Every night, the moon grew smaller and smaller until only a tiny crescent was left.

'What shall we do, what shall we do?' chattered the Meerkats, terrified by the sight of the disappearing moon. 'We need to stop the lolloping-long-legs before he can eat the whole thing.'

Umberto continued to graze, unworried and unhurried by the minuscule mammals beneath him.

The next night, the mischievous Meerkats hatched a plan. They would save the moon from the slumbering sleepwalker and the elders would treat them with respect for once.

Umberto stretched his sinuous structure, aware of the emptiness of his stomach. The sky was dark, the rumble of thunder echoed over the plains as rain began to fall onto the parched prairies.

Prairies: Places which are normally flat, have lots of grasses and very few trees.

Umberto enjoyed the snake of water that trickled from the hairs on his horns to the hooves of his feet. The rainy season had come and the leaves would be so much sweeter.

The blackness of the clouds had hidden the moon but Umberto could smell the tender tips regardless of the deluge, his stomach rumbled.

Ears alert, the Meerkats scampered from the ground, on an urgent mission to save the moon.

One stopped so suddenly the other bumped into him, hard enough they both ended up in a muddy mess. 'We're too late!' They scanned the sky but there wasn't a star to be found, or the moon.

Umberto had finally finished his feast when he felt
something scamper up his leg. And then another.
Something was jumping up and down on his back,
then on his neck until finally; two furious furry
friends came eye to eye with him.

'Put it back!' one ordered.

'It's not yours.' said the other.

The miserable Meerkats looked at the sky and then

at each other. 'Why did you eat the moon?'

Umberto laughed and laughed, and shook and

laughed. In fact he laughed so much that the

minuscule mammals had trouble holding onto the

small mane that ran down his neck. 'I didn't eat

the moon.'

'Yes you did!' said one Meerkat.

'You ate a bit every night until it was all gone.' sobbed the other.

Umberto looked at the muddy mammals. 'I didn't eat the moon at all.'

'Then where is it?' asked the puzzled pair.

Umberto looked up at the sky and wondered that himself. He hadn't eaten the moon, had he?

Just then clouds parted and the moon broke through, the lunar lantern was back.

The minuscule mammals jumped up and down cheering, it was then they who spotted the brown splodges of mud they had covered the long-lashed leggy creature with.

'What a relief.' Umberto blinked, his long neck stretched so he could talk to the creatures that sat between his shoulder blades.

Neither Meerkat wanted to admit their mistake, but once the story had been told, Umberto's laugh echoed on the equator and the troublesome two? They scampered back to the safety of their burrow, ashamed that they had misjudged Umberto.

Tired and full Umberto settled down to sleep, unaware of the muddy mess the meddlesome Meerkats had left him in.

And in the morning?

Well, let's just say that the giraffe that woke up
looked just like the creatures that roam the plains
now.

Dear Reader

I hope you have enjoyed reading how Umberto go his spots. Do you think he looks better with them? I hope you enjoyed learning some new words too.

If you liked reading 'How the Giraffe got his Spots' why not look out for my other story, 'Woolly Pig's Woolly Jumper.' Also available on Amazon.

If you have liked reading my book then please tell your friends and relatives and leave a review on Amazon.
Thank you.

Sandra xx

The Author

Born in Lowestoft, Sandra Joanne Forder always wanted to be an author, publishing a book of poetry aged seventeen under her maiden name of Sandra James. The book called Teenage Years was locally published. Since then Sandra had written many books but has never published anything until Woolly Pig's Woolly Jumper which came out in October 2016. Look out for new titles coming in the near future.

If you would like to know more about Sandra and to follow her on social media please go to

https://www.facebook.com/sandrajoanneforder

Printed in Great Britain
by Amazon